Lying UP a STORM

published by

NATIONAL CENTER for
YOUTH ISSUES

www.ncyi.org

*For the little storms
brewing in all of us!*

-Julia

DUPLICATION AND COPYRIGHT

NATIONAL CENTER for
YOUTH ISSUES

P.O. Box 22185
Chattanooga, TN 37422-2185
423.899.5714 • 866.318.6294
fax: 423.899.4547 • www.ncyi.org

ISBN: 978-1-937870-34-8 $9.95
© 2015 National Center for Youth Issues, Chattanooga, TN
All rights reserved.
Written by: Julia Cook
Illustrations by: Michelle Hazelwood Hyde
Design by: Phillip W. Rodgers
Contributing Editors: Beth Spencer Rabon and Jennifer Deshler
Published by National Center for Youth Issues • Softcover
Printed at Starkey Printing, Chattanooga, Tennessee, U.S.A., May 2018

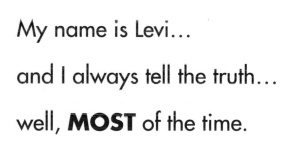

My name is Levi…

and I always tell the truth…

well, **MOST** of the time.

4

Whenever I don't like the truth, I kinda, sorta make up other stuff to say. Sometimes the truth is boring, and sometimes it's just easier to tell people what they want to hear. Sometimes, lying keeps me from getting in trouble.

Besides, it's not like I tell great, big,

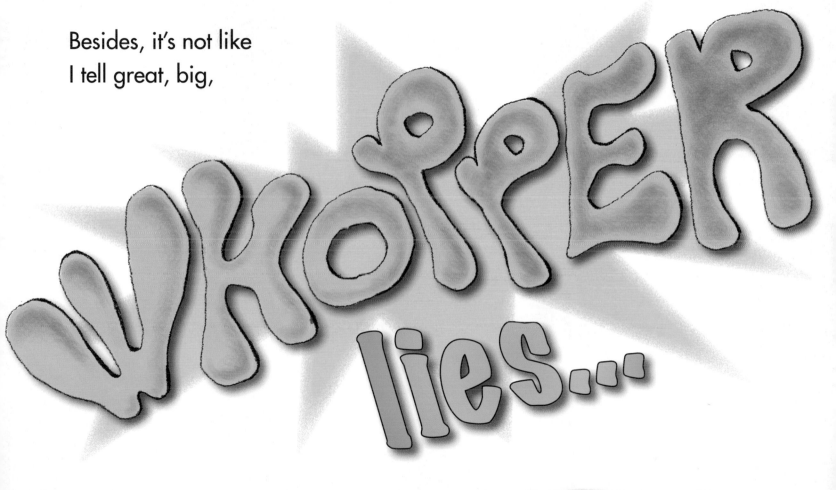

I just tell itty bitty ones.

Last night, I had homework to do, but I accidentally left it in my desk at school. When I got home, my mom asked me,

"Levi, do you have homework tonight?"

I had to think really quick on my feet,
and come up with a story that she would believe.
I didn't have my homework, but I couldn't tell her why,
so I decided to tell an itty bitty lie.

"We didn't have any." (I think it worked.)

This morning when I got to school, my teacher asked me,
"Levi, where is your homework?"

I had to think really quick on my feet.
If I told her the truth, my teacher would freak!
I didn't do my homework, but I couldn't tell her why,
so I decided to tell another tiny lie.

"I left it at home."
(I think it worked!)

At recess, all of the cool kids were talking about where they have been and where they are going.

"We're going to New York City over Thanksgiving break!"

"We're going on a cruise to the Bahamas over winter break!"

"We did that last year. This year we're going skiing in Utah!"

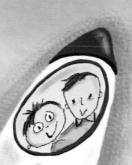

I had to think really quick on my feet.
I just didn't want to seem like a geek.
I looked down at the dirt, and up at the sky,
and then I came up with a great, big FAT lie
(almost a whopper!)

"My Uncle Jim is going to be one of the first
people to spend a week on the moon, and he
told me I could go with him."

"Nuh Uh..."
"Yeah Right, Levi...
or, should we call
you 'Le-LIE?'"

(I don't think
that one worked
very well.)

9

The rest of my day went pretty well. I only had to lie a few more times.

Bingo!

"...Levi, I've only called 3 numbers."

"But this is MY pencil. I brought it from home. My grandma's name is Edith and she gave this pencil to me last week, I promise!"

"Yeah right, 'Le-LIE.'"

"Nope, it wasn't me. I never log onto that game site at school. I was just doing my math."

"Yeah right, 'Le-LIE.'"

"I didn't do it, I promise.

It must have been that bumble bee!"

"Really??"

"Yeah right, 'Le-LIE.'"

"I'm pretty sure that's not what happened," my teacher said.

At the end of the day, my teacher handed me a note.

"Make sure your mom gets this, Levi."

"OK, I will."

"How was your day?"

"Good."

"Your teacher called and said to expect a note from her. Do you have it?"

I had to think really quick on my feet.
If I told the truth, my mom would just freak!
I threw the note away, but I couldn't tell her why,
so I decided to tell another little lie.

"I can't find it. I think it must have fallen out
of my backpack on the way home from school."

"Are you sure?"

YEP!

At first, I thought it had worked, but then my mom said,

"Levi, when you tell a lie,
your inside sun goes away.

Then a lying cloud forms,
and glooms up your day.

Telling one lie leads to telling another.

You've lied to
your teacher,

your friends, and your mother.

You've lied at school.

You've lied at home,

and right now son, you're lying up a **storm!!!**"

"But Mom!"

"There are no buts about it!
Levi, you've been caught.
You must start telling the truth,
and this lying has to STOP!"

STOP

"I realize you might think
It's easier to lie.
But telling lies will hurt you,
and let me tell you why."

"Whenever you tell a lie, your inside sun goes away.
Then a lying cloud forms, and glooms up your day.

Each time you tell a lie, another cloud starts to form,
and before you can stop it from happening, your insides start to storm."

"Lying causes your friends not to trust you.
They'll start to push you away.
And then you'll feel all alone,
because no one will want to play."

"Mom, do you ever lie?"

"Yes, I have told lies before.
Just last week, I told the man at the movie booth that you were two years younger than you actually are so I could pay less for your ticket."

"But when I sat down to watch the movie,
my inside sun went away.
Clouds came in and made me feel bad,
and it just about ruined my day."

"I got out of my seat and went to the man sitting at the ticket booth.
I paid him the extra money, and then told him the truth.

I started to feel
much better inside,
and my storm
cleared up right away.

I told the truth
even though
it was hard,
then I had a
much better day."

"Levi, people lie all the time for a lot of different reasons, but that doesn't make it right!

You can't do anything about other people lying...you can only control what YOU do. But I know for sure that you won't ever be happy if you don't have an inside sun.

I know you don't like
your stormy inside,
and if you want it
to go away,
don't lie to yourself
and others.

Tell the truth...
and start today!"

I felt really awful! Not only was I lying to others, I was lying to ME!
My heart was wet and soggy, and I hadn't seen my inside sun for days.
I decided to give telling the truth a try.

"Mom, I lied to you about the note.
I threw it in the trash can so I
wouldn't get in trouble."

"Thank you Levi, for
telling me the truth!"

(Wow! She didn't
freak out...not even
a little bit!)

The next day at school, I told my teacher the truth…about a lot of things.

"I'm sorry I lied…It was me that logged onto that video game site during math yesterday."

"Thank you Levi, for telling me the truth!"

"Oh, and I was the one who knocked over your vase. It wasn't a bumble bee."

"Thank you Levi, for telling me the truth!"

"Oh, and I really didn't have a Bingo yesterday…I just wanted to win!"

"Thank you Levi, for telling me the truth!"

(My teacher didn't freak out. I was shocked.)

At recess, I told the cool kids that I'd lied about my
Uncle Jim going to the moon, and then said I was sorry.

"It's ok Levi. Want to play football with us at recess?"

(They didn't freak out either.)

Just before the bell rang, I told Edith the truth
about her pencil, and then gave it back to her.

She **TOTALLY** freaked out on me!!!

...Figures!

By the time I got home,
my storm was gone.
My mom was right.
Lying feels wrong.

From now on I'll know
what I need to do.
No matter how hard it is,
I'm telling the truth!

"Levi, did you wash your hands?"

"YEP...NOPE!

I'll go do it right now!"

Advice for Parents & Educators

When a child tells a lie, it does not mean they are headed for a life of delinquency. Lying is a normal, expected behavior in children. In fact, it is actually a sign of healthy brain development. When children lie, they are developing invaluable social skills…they are recognizing that other people may not have the same beliefs and feelings they do. To lie, children must effectively use their executive function skill set which involves working memory, inhibitory control, and planning capabilities. They must effectively hide what actually happens, develop and plan an alternate reality, explain that reality effectively, and remember that reality for future recall.

Most often, children lie to cover up their mistakes and avoid getting punished. Immature inhibitory control leads to poor choice making. Children don't want to suffer the consequences, so lying becomes an attractive alternative.

There are things; however, that parents, educators and care takers can do to foster honesty in children:

1. Don't invite the child to lie by asking a question. Instead, make a corrective statement and move on. (i.e. Instead of asking the child, "Did you leave the door open?" say "I know you left the door open. Try to remember to shut it next time.")

2. Before questioning a child about an incident, ask him/her to promise to tell you the truth. Making a promise to someone you care about makes telling a lie more difficult.

3. Do NOT tell a lie! If you promise not to get angry or promise not to give consequences if your child tells the truth, do not go back on your word. This will only encourage your child to lie to

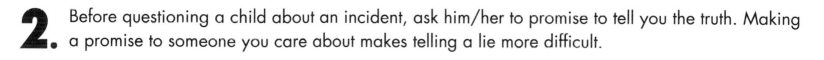

you in the future. Instead, **compliment your child for being honest** with you and ignore the misbehavior, or promise to lessen the consequences if the behavior is too severe to ignore.

4. There may be times when you want your children to lie, (i.e. if they answer the phone when you are not home and they tell the person you are in the shower.) Discuss circumstances when telling a lie can help to keep your children safe, and explain why it is OK to lie in certain circumstances.

5. Be honest yourself. It is very hard to convince your children not to lie if they see you doing it.

6. Help children understand that mistakes are learning opportunities, and if they blame others for their mistakes, they give away their opportunities to learn. Making mistakes does not make you a bad person, so you don't need to lie to cover them up.

7. Respect your child's right to privacy when they don't want to share with you.

8. Let your children know they are loved unconditionally. Always separate what they do from who they are.

9. Change your "buts" to "ands." "Today you had a rough day, **and** tomorrow is a brand new day! I can't wait to see what you can do with your tomorrow." This will validate your recognition of their behavior to a higher degree.

10. Stop trying to control your child. Many children lie so they can find out who they are and what they want to do. They are also lying to please others by making them believe they are doing what they are supposed to do.

11. Focus on building trust and communication with children instead of focusing on the behavior problem. This is the quickest way to diminish the misbehavior.